MINI MEGA

ACTIVITY BOOK

Have **FUN** completing this mini book
FILLED with >**1,000**< **MEGA** activities!

PUZZLE over **PRINCESSES**,
COLOR the **HOOT-IFUL OWLS**,
and **EXPRESS** yourself with **EMOTIS**.

With over **500 STICKERS** to use
in the **BOOK** or wherever you want!

make
believe
ideas

PLAYFUL PUP

Find and circle **FOUR THINGS** beginning with **P**.

INTO THE WOODS

Start

5 Help **OLIVIA** the **OWL** find the way to her **NEST**.
Make sure to **AVOID** the **OBSTACLES**.

6 **COLOR** the **TREES**.

Finish

7 **HOW MANY** **DEER** can you **COUNT**? **WRITE** the ANSWER: ....

8 **COLOR** the **EGGS**.

3

HIDE AND SEEK

LOOK at the SCENE.
✓ the BOXES
when you **FIND** the
ANIMALS on the list.

9 1 cat ✓

10 1 sheep ✓

11 2 chicks ✓

12 2 frogs ✓

13  3 bees ✓

14  3 owls ✓

15 4 ladybugs ✓

16  5 mice ✓

5

SPELLING BEE

17 buzz

HELP **BETTY** the **BEE** TRACE the **WORDS**.

18 flower

19 spring

20 COPY the **FLOWER**. Use the GRID to help you.

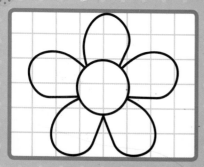

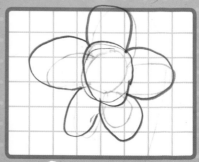

21 Now **COLOR** it in.

6

TASTY TREATS

COLOR the ICE-CREAMS to MATCH the YUMMY FLAVORS.

VANILLA

 CHOCOLATE

STRAWBERRY

 MINT

DOODLE some COOL PATTERNS on the cones.

DRAW TASTY TOPPINGS on the ICE-CREAMS.

WALL OF FAME

DRAW or **ATTACH** pictures of your FRIENDS
that **MATCH** the DESCRIPTIONS **BELOW.**

31 most adventurous

32 smartest

33 coolest

34 most artistic

35 most embarrassing

36 sweetest

37 funniest

8

PRINCESS PATH

38 GUIDE the PRINCESS through the **MAZE** to the PONY.

Start

Finish

40 COLOR the **PALACE**.

39 **HOW MANY** FLOWERS can you count? WRITE the **ANSWER:** ....

SUMMER STYLE

MATCH the **SWIMSUITS** to the correct COLORED SUNGLASSES.

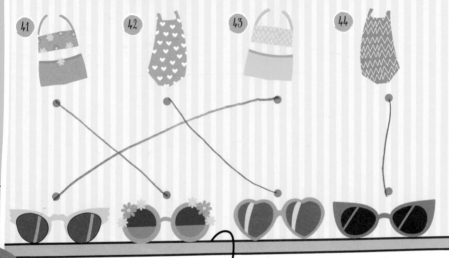

41 42 43 44

45 JOIN the **DOTS** to finish the **DRESS**.

Use **COLOR** to finish the PATTERNS.

46

47

48

SHADOW MATCHER

MATCH each **OWL** to its SHADOW.

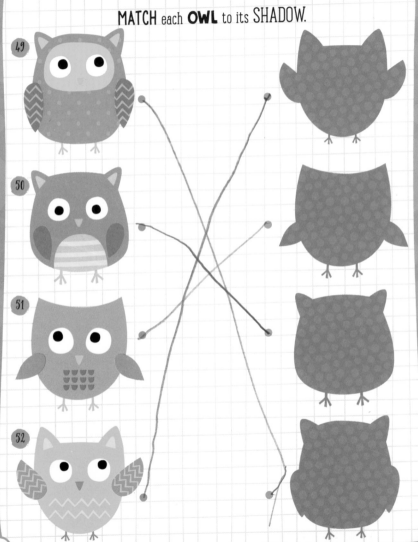

49

50

51

52

CROWN TOWN

The **PRINCESS** is **SHOPPING** for a **NEW CROWN!**
FIND the thing that **DOESN'T BELONG** on each **SHELF.**

53

54

55

56

57 **HOW MANY** BLUE **JEWELS** can you count?
WRITE the **ANSWER:** ....

WHO'S WHO?

CIRCLE the **ANSWERS** to each question.

58 **WHO** doesn't have **WINGS**?

59 **WHO DOESN'T** belong in **WATER**?

60 **WHICH** of these is not a **FRUIT**?

61 **WHAT** likes the **COLD**?

62 **WHAT** do you wear on your **FEET**?

IMAGINE EMOTIS

DOODLE an **EMOTI** for the things below.

63 SLEEPOVER

64 SCHOOL

65 THE BEACH

66 CAMPING

PERFECT PICNIC

TRACE the **LINES** to see what the **PRINCESSES** are bringing to their **PICNIC**.

68

69

70

71

72

73 Now **COLOR** them in.

74 **DECORATE** the picnic BLANKET with pretty **PATTERNS**.

OWL SUMS

Help **OSCAR** the **OWL** finish the SUMS.

75) 2 + 2 = 4

76) 2 + 4 = 6

77) 2 − 1 = 1

78) 4 − 2 = 2

79) 3 + 2 = 5

80) 3 + 4 = 7

81) 3 + 3 = 6

82) 4 + 4 = 8

83) 3 − 1 = 2

84) 4 − 3 = 1

MY FAMILY

In the **FRAMES**, draw members of your **FAMILY** as **EMOTIS**.
Then **WRITE** their **FAVORITE THINGS** below.

85

87

86 Favorite food:

....

88 Favorite drink:

....

89

91

90 Favorite color:

....

92 Favorite movie:

....

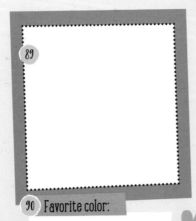

93

94 Favorite song:

....

95

96 Favorite place:

....

97

98 Favorite book:

....

99

100 Favorite animal:

....

19

PRETTY PURSES

101 Use the **NUMBERS** in the **FLOWERS** as a guide to **COLOR** the PURSE.

102 Find **EIGHT** matching **PAIRS**.

103

104

DOODLE pretty **PATTERNS** on the **PURSES.**

105

106

107

108 Finish the **CHARM.**

21

TWIT-TWOO TRACE

109 flight

TRACE the LETTERS to help the **OWLS** spell the WORDS.

110 night

111 wing

112 wise

113 COLOR the **OWL**.

 # EMOTI HAPPY

DESIGN your own **EMOTIS** for the things that make you SMILE.
Then **WRITE** the NAME of the thing in the space beneath each FRAME.

PLACES

114

115

PEOPLE

116

117

FOOD

118

119

HOBBIES

120

121

23

FLYING FRIENDS

Can you find TEN **DIFFERENCES** between the SCENES?

HEAD-TO-TOE LOOKS

132 DESIGN a beautiful **DRESS**.

133 DECORATE the **HAT**.

134 TRACE the LINES to complete the **BAG**.

135 Use the **NUMBERS** in the key as a guide to **COLOR** the SHOES.

 1 2 3

JAZZY GEMS

136 COLOR the RING.

FIND the **WORDS** in the **WORD SEARCH**. **WORDS** can go **DOWN** or **ACROSS**.

d	o	w	v	c	e	n	e	c	l
t	o	l	s	h	g	e	m	r	s
d	r	a	f	x	z	r	e	m	a
i	p	r	u	b	y	u	r	m	p
a	p	y	s	p	p	i	a	r	p
m	q	u	i	v	i	o	l	s	h
o	t	w	l	g	o	l	d	r	i
n	y	i	v	o	a	d	s	f	r
d	g	j	e	k	s	h	i	n	e
l	c	v	n	b	n	d	o	y	p

137 diamond ✓

138 emerald ✓

139 gem ✓

140 gold ✓

141 ruby ✓

142 sapphire ✓

143 shine ✓

144 silver ✓

145 **HOW MANY** **GEMS** are there? **WRITE** the **ANSWER:** ....

MINI MAKEOVERS

146 beach babe

Give each **GIRL** an amazing **HAIRSTYLE** for her **VACATION**.

147 spa trip

148 city break

149 polar trek

150 safari

BEAUTIFUL BEDROOM

151 Can you **FIND** the cuddly **DINOSAUR?**

152 COLOR the **BED**.

Find **FOUR TIARAS.** ✓ the **BOXES** when you **FIND** them.

153 1   154 2   155 3   156 4

T-SHIRT CHALLENGE

157 **DOODLE** and **DESIGN** cool **MOTIFS** that could go on a **T-SHIRT**.

158 Now use **COLOR** to make them **STAND OUT** on the page.

Use the **GRIDS** to
finish the **T-SHIRTS**.

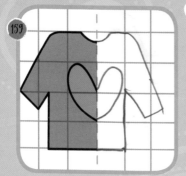
159

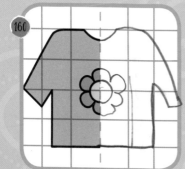
160

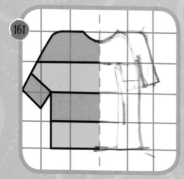
161

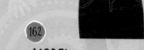
162

Give the **MODEL** a
COOL T-shirt.

SUMMERTIME

SUNNY the **OWL** has been on HOLIDAY.
163 **DOODLE** a PICTURE on the **POSTCARD**.

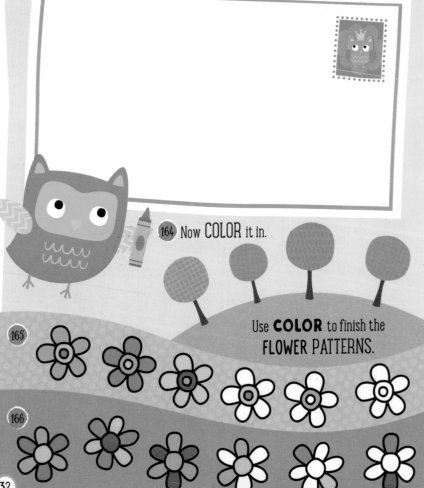

164 Now COLOR it in.

Use **COLOR** to finish the **FLOWER PATTERNS**.

165

166

PUTTING ON THE GLITZ

167 Guide **CHARLIE** through the **MAZE** to reach her ACCESSORIES!

Finish

Start

168

169

COLOR the cool **CUFF** and EARRINGS.

TIME TO TRACE

TRACE the LETTERS to help **PEPPER** the **PONY** spell the WORDS.

170 apple

171 pony

172 ride

173 hay

174 COLOR **PEPPER.**

TROPICAL TEASER

FIND and **CIRCLE** the **THREE** items
that look **EXACTLY** like these ones.

175   176   177

FIND THE DIFFERENCE

Can you find **FIVE DIFFERENCES** between the **SCENES?**

✔ the **BOXES** when you **FIND** them.

 178 | 1   179 | 2   180 | 3   181 | 4   182 | 5

36

OWLTASTIC ART

COLOR the OWLS.

188 **HOW MANY** LADYBUGS can you count? WRITE the **ANSWER**:

SUNNY DAYDREAMS

FIND the **WORDS** in the **WORD SEARCH**. **WORDS** can go DOWN or **ACROSS**.

d	r	e	s	s	c	h	f	r
r	s	a	g	u	s	i	l	e
u	u	r	z	n	w	o	o	b
t	n	r	h	g	t	y	w	e
t	h	i	y	l	l	a	e	a
s	a	n	d	a	l	s	r	c
x	t	g	x	s	v	r	s	h
e	f	s	s	s	j	p	o	k
b	u	t	t	e	r	f	l	y
b	a	z	q	s	w	a	g	o

189 beach

190 butterfly

191 dress

192 earrings

193 flowers

194 sandals

195 sunglasses

196 sun hat

197 **COLOR** the **BUTTERFLIES**.

38

DELICIOUS DUOS

Draw LINES to MATCH the CUPCAKES.

198 199 200 201

SUPER SKETCHES

202 COPY the **PURSE**. Use the GRID to help you.

203 Now **COLOR** it to MATCH.

204 HOW MANY PENCILS can you count? WRITE the **ANSWER**: ....

205 COPY the **SUNGLASSES**. Use the GRID to help you.

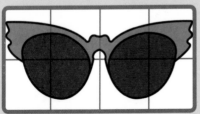

206 Now **COLOR** them to MATCH.

ROYAL BALL

207 **DECORATE** the **OUTFITS** for the **ROYAL** GUESTS.

208 **COLOR** the **INVITATION**.

EMOTI SLEEPOVER

DESIGN **EMOTI** PAJAMAS for **YOU** and your **FRIENDS** to wear at a **SLEEPOVER!**

209

210

211 COLOR the **FUN** ACTIVITIES.

212 NOW CIRCLE your **FAVORITE**.

213 DOODLE **EMOTIS** on the OVERNIGHT KNAPSACK.

214 COLOR the tasty **SNACKS**.

215 CIRCLE your top three SNACKS.

FOREST FUN

216 Help **OLIVER** the **OWL** through the **MAZE** to reach his friend, **OSCAR**.

Start

218 COLOR the **OWL** FRIENDS.

217 **HOW MANY** STARS can you count? WRITE the **ANSWER:** ....

Finish

SHOE SEARCH

Find and CIRCLE **FOUR** BALLERINA SHOES.

✔ the **BOXES** when you **FIND** them.

219 1   220 2   221 3   222 4

NAME GAME

DRAW a LINE to connect the **OWLS** to their NAMES.

223

NOISY NINA

224

BEAUTIFUL BONNIE

225

WORRIED WENDY

SLEEPY SIMON

226

227 COLOR the **OWLS**.

MAKE A STATEMENT

DOODLE **EMOTI** BEADS and **CHARMS** to CREATE unique **NECKLACES**.

WOODLAND WALK

COLOR the **WOODLAND** THINGS to complete the **PATTERNS**.

234

235

236

237

238

TIME FOR TEA

DECORATE the TEACUPS with pretty **PATTERNS**.

239

240

241

242

243 CIRCLE the **CUPCAKE** that is DIFFERENT.

WHAT A HOOT

TRACE the LETTERS to find out
what each **BIRD** is saying.

244 hoot

245 tweet

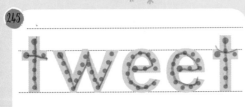

246 squawk

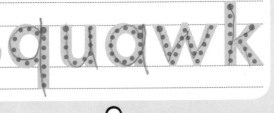

247 chirp

248 COLOR the **FLOWERS**.

STYLISH SHIPWRECK

FIND the **WORDS** in the WORD SEARCH. **WORDS** can go DOWN or **ACROSS**.

a	t	q	o	y	s	n	n
s	h	b	a	g	r	s	i
w	q	e	n	t	m	c	n
s	u	l	b	d	c	b	g
h	a	t	l	s	s	o	a
o	e	i	t	d	a	o	p
e	r	i	c	o	a	t	n
c	a	o	y	s	r	l	t
d	r	e	s	s	a	e	i
u	t	x	o	y	y	p	w

249 bag ✓

250 belt ✓

251 boot ✓

252 coat ✓

253 dress ✓

254 hat ✓

255 ring ✓

256 shoe ✓

DRAW the things you'd need if you were **SHIPWRECKED** on an **ISLAND!**

257

258

259

260

51

MY FRIENDS

In the **FRAMES**, draw your FRIENDS as EMOTIS.
Then write their **NAMES** below each frame.

261

262

263

264

265

266

267

268

269

270

271

272

273

274

275

276

53

BELLE OF THE BALL

277 CONNECT the **DOTS** to finish the **CROWN**.

278 COLOR the **SHOES**.

279 COLOR the princess **DRESS**. Use the **COLORED DOTS** as a GUIDE.

280 COLOR the **PUPPY**.

EMOTI-MATH

Finish the **EMOTI** SUMS.

281   1 + 5 = 6

286   5 + 2 = 7

282   7 - 4 = 3

287   10 - 9 = 1

283   8 + 2 = 6

288   4 + 4 = 8

284   1 + 1 = 2

289   6 + 3 = 9

285   6 - 2 = 4

290   8 - 4 = 4

GORGEOUS GEMS

TRACE the LINES to reveal the GORGEOUS **GEMS**.

291 **SAPPHIRE**

292 Then COLOR it **BLUE.**

293 **EMERALD**

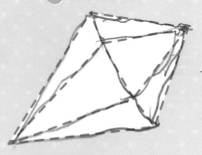

294 Then COLOR it **GREEN.**

295 **RUBY**

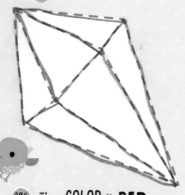

296 Then COLOR it **RED.**

297 **AMBER**

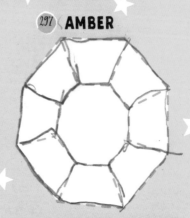

298 Then COLOR it **ORANGE.**

FIND THE ONE

FIND and **CIRCLE** the **FOUR OWLS** that look **EXACTLY** like these ones:

299
300
301
302

303 Now **DRAW** a **STAR** around **YOUR FAVORITE OWL**.

PALACE GARDENS

304 COLOR the **PALACE**.

305 DESIGN a **FLAG**.

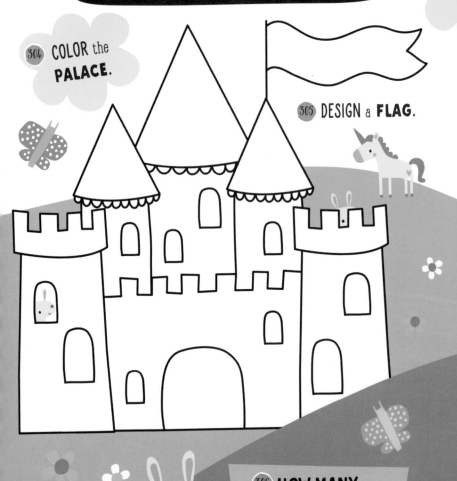

306 **HOW MANY** BUNNIES can you count? WRITE the **ANSWER**: ....

TRACE the BUTTERFLY TRAILS.

Use **COLOR** to finish
the **FLOWER** PATTERNS.

308

309

310

SWEET DREAMS

311 DOODLE what you think OTIS the OWL is **DREAMING** about.

312 Then **COLOR** it in.

313 TRACE the LINES to reveal what OKI the OWL is **DREAMING** about.

314 Then **COLOR** it in.

PHOTO FRENZY

315 Follow the LINES to help EMILY pick up CARA.

316 COLOR the CAR.

317 COLOR ELLIE'S beautiful DRESS.

318 CONNECT the DOTS to finish the CAMERA.

MATCH THE OWL

319 DOODLE details on the **PLAIN OWL** to make it MATCH the OWL at the **TOP!**

320 COLOR the **STARS**.

321 TRACE the LINES to finish the **LEAVES**.

322 Then **COLOR** them in.

323 **HOW MANY** STARS can you count? WRITE the **ANSWER:** ....

GEEK CHIC

324 FIND and **CIRCLE** FIVE differences between the **KNAPSACKS**.

Draw **LINES** to match the **GIRLS** to their **ACCESSORIES**.

STUNNING SUNFLOWERS

328 **CIRCLE** the **TALLEST** SUNFLOWER.

329 TRACE the **DOTS** to **FINISH** the SUNFLOWER STEMS.

330 COLOR the **TROPHY**.

331 **DOODLE** PATTERNS on the **PLANT POTS**.

PUTTING ON A SHOW

332 Can you **HELP** the **SINGER** find her lost MICROPHONE?

Start

Finish

333 COLOR the audience EMOTIS.

SUPER STARS

334 TRACE the **DOTS** to create PATTERNS in the night sky.

335 **COLOR** DAPHNE the DEER.

336 **CIRCLE** the FLOWER that doesn't **BELONG**.

Follow the **LINES** to see which **NEST** belongs to who.

337

338

339

340 COLOR the **BIRDS** to **MATCH** their **EGGS.**

ENCHANTED FOREST

DRAW **LINES** to MATCH the **PAIRS**.

341

342

343

344

345 **DOODLE** some LEAVES on the **PATH**.

ACCESSORY STYLE

Use **COLOR** to complete the **STYLISH** PATTERNS.

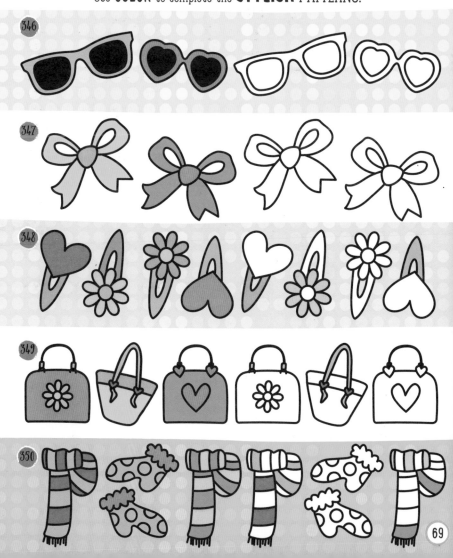

EMOTI FUN

COPY the **EMOTIS.** Use the GRIDS to help you.

351

352

353

354 Now **COLOR** them in.

GROOVY GIRL

FIND and **CIRCLE** the **FOUR** items that look **EXACTLY** like these ones:

 355

356

357

 358

SECRET GARDEN

Use COLOR to FINISH the FLOWER PATTERNS.

359

360

361

REARRANGE the LETTERS
to make GARDEN words.

DPNO

362 ....

TCAUSC

363 ....

72

Use the **GRIDS** to **FINISH** the FLOWERS.

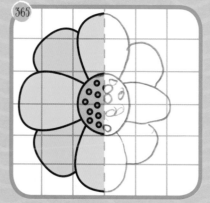

366 NOW COLOR them in!

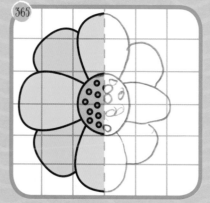

367 FINISH the WEATHER **EMOTIS** and CIRCLE the top TWO that will help your GARDEN GROW.

SLEEPOVER STYLE

Search the **GRID** for the SLEEPOVER words below.
WORDS can go DOWN or **ACROSS**.

✔ each WORD when you've **FOUND** IT.

a	m	f	p	p	i	l	q	s	s
n	o	g	q	s	d	x	d	l	o
i	v	w	n	x	r	o	i	e	p
g	i	s	o	b	e	d	g	e	i
h	e	k	y	x	a	t	h	p	l
t	p	w	s	d	m	a	s	s	l
e	p	o	p	c	o	r	n	n	o
m	a	k	e	o	v	e	r	a	w
l	e	q	w	u	g	q	u	c	d
n	z	v	b	b	o	o	k	k	a

368 bed ☐

369 book ☐

370 dream ☐

371 movie ☐

372 makeover ☐

373 night ☐

374 pillow ☐

375 popcorn ☐

376 sleep ☐

377 snack ☐

378 DRAW your **BEST** DREAM:

74

PERFECT PALACE

379 TRACE the BUTTERFLY trail.

380 **HOW MANY** STARS are there? WRITE the **ANSWER:** ....

381 COLOR the PALACE.

382 CIRCLE the PRINCESS that is DIFFERENT.

75

EMOTI PAIRS

Draw **LINES** to **JOIN** the **PAIRS** of **EMOTIS**.

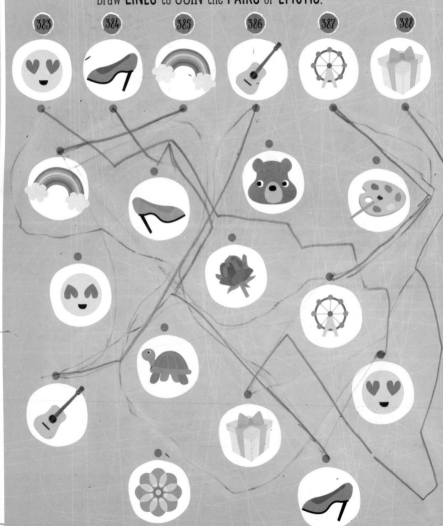

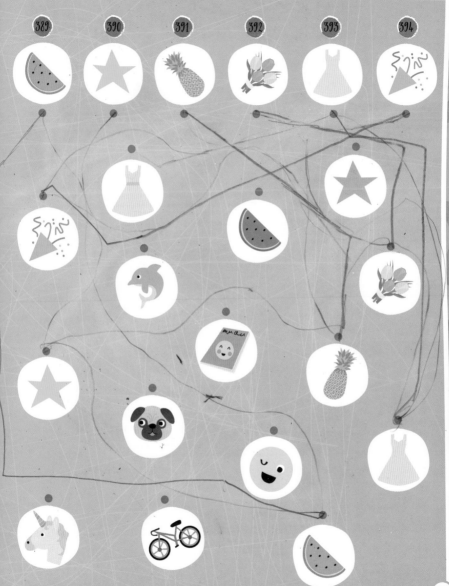

FILL THE FRAMES

395 COLOR the **PRINCESS**.

396 DRAW a **TIARA** for the PRINCESS.

397 DESIGN a BEAUTIFUL
HAIRDO for the PRINCESS.

398 DRAW YOURSELF
as a **PRINCESS**.

GUESS WHO?

399 **TRACE** the **DOTS** to **COMPLETE** the **PICTURE**.

400 Then **COLOR** it in.

401 Can you **FIND** the **BABY** OWL?

402 **DOODLE** LEAVES and **TWIGS** in the **NEST**.

JEWEL FOREST

LOOK at the SCENE.
the **BOXES** when you **FIND**
the THINGS on the list.

403
2 blue jewels ✓

404
2 pink jewels ✓

405
3 ladybugs ✓

406
1 purple jewel ✓

407
3 green jewels ✓

408
1 crown ✓

409 COLOR the PRINCESS.

410 DRAW some more **TOADSTOOLS** in the FOREST.

81

EMOTI STYLE
CREATE **EMOTI DESIGNS** for these beautiful OUTFITS.

411

412

Draw **LINES** to MATCH the **DRESSES** to the **CORRECT COLORED** SHOES.

413

414

415

416

WINTER STYLE

417 Use the **KEY** below as a guide to COLOR the **WINTER WOOLLIES**.

| 1 | 2 | 3 | 4 |

418 DOODLE a **DESIGN** on the WOOL HAT.

419 CONNECT the **DOTS** to finish the **COAT**. **420** Now **COLOR** it in.

84

CIRCLE the one that DOESN'T BELONG on each SHELF.

421

422

423

DESIGN some BOOTS and a CLUTCH BAG.

424

425

EMOTI ART

COPY the **EMOTIS**. Use the GRIDS to help you.

426

427

428

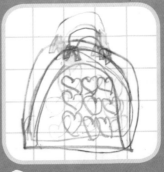

429 Now **COLOR** them in.

SHOPPING SPREE

SOPHIE has been on a **SHOPPING SPREE!** Finish the **SUMS**.

430 7 + 3 = 10

435 11 - 2 = 9

431 2 + 4 = 6

436 8 - 5 = 3

432 3 + 2 = 5

437 1 + 3 = 4

433 4 + 4 = 8

438 10 - 9 = 1

434 6 + 1 = 7

439 9 - 7 = 4

SILLY SCENE

This SCENE isn't RIGHT!
CIRCLE the **EIGHT** things that **DON'T BELONG.**

✔ the boxes when you **FIND** them.

440 [1]   441 [2]   442 [3]   443 [4]

444 [5]   445 [6]   446 [7]   447 [8]

448 Use **COLOR** to complete the **SCENE.**

449 Can you FIND NINE LADYBUGS?

TROPICAL FISH

Rearrange the **LETTERS** to make **OCEAN** WORDS.

POTOUSC

450 ....

HLEWA

451 ....

COMPLETE the **FISH PATTERNS** using **BRIGHT** COLORS.

452

453

454

455

90

RED CARPET

Can you find **FIVE DIFFERENCES** between the **SCENES**?

✓ the **BOXES** when you **FIND** them.

 456 | 1 | 457 | 2 | 458 | 3 | 459 | 4 | 460 | 5

WINTER WONDERLAND

461 Give the **SNOWMAN** a SPARKLING CROWN.

462

DRAW the SNOWMAN
a **CARROT NOSE.**

463 DECORATE the
PRINCESS' **COAT.**

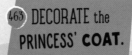

464 COLOR the MITTENS.

465 Can you **FIND** the PLAYFUL PENGUIN?

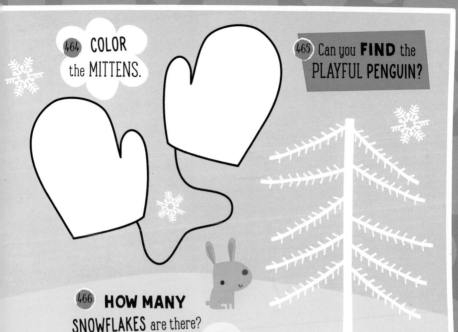

466 **HOW MANY** SNOWFLAKES are there? WRITE the **ANSWER**: ....

467 COPY the **WINTER PALACE**. Use the GRIDS to help you.

468 Now **COLOR** it in.

SUPER SUNDAE

FOLLOW each **LINE** to see who gets to eat the **SUPER SUNDAE**.

469

470

471

472 ✔ the **BOXES** to **DESIGN** your **PERFECT ICE-CREAM SUNDAE**.

- [ ] cherries
- [ ] chocolate
- [ ] raspberry sauce
- [ ] sprinkles
- [ ] toffee sauce
- [ ] wafer

473 COLOR the TASTY **TREAT**.

BUSY BEACH

FIND the **WORDS** in the WORD SEARCH. WORDS can go **DOWN** or **ACROSS**.

x	w	r	a	b	d	g	h
p	a	l	m	t	r	e	e
w	t	o	o	h	a	s	k
s	e	e	u	u	b	h	f
a	r	n	p	y	r	e	i
r	m	z	o	s	a	l	s
s	e	a	g	u	l	l	h
q	l	r	e	n	x	h	q
c	o	c	o	n	u	t	r
w	n	u	a	s	d	p	t

474 coconut ✓

475 crab ✓

476 fish ✓

477 palm tree

478 seagull ✓

479 shell ✓

480 sun ✓

481 watermelon

DRAW EMOTIS of THREE ANIMALS you might find on a **BEACH**.

482

483

484

HOME, SWEET HOME

485 DRAW the **HOUSE** you live in.

486 Now **COLOR** it in.

487 DESIGN a COOL **KEYRING**.

488 Now **COLOR** it in.

489 COLOR the BUTTERFLIES.

490 DESIGN your **DREAM** HOME.

ROYAL BANQUET

READ the **CHEF'S LIST** and CIRCLE the items on the SHELVES.

CHEF'S LIST

491 cherries

492 chocolate

493 eggs

494 jelly

495 **CIRCLE** the LOLLIPOP that doesn't **MATCH**.

496 **COLOR** the CHEF'S **APRON**.

FEATHER FASHION

The OWLS are having a **FASHION SHOW**.
DOODLE **DETAILS** on the OWLS to make them look BEAUTIFUL.

PAJAMA PARTY

501 **DESIGN** the ULTIMATE SLIPPERS.

Which PAJAMAS will each girl **WEAR**?
FOLLOW the LINES to find out.

502

503

504 Now **DESIGN** some PAJAMAS.

505 **DRAW** a MIDNIGHT SNACK.

506 **DESIGN** a COOL **OVERNIGHT BAG.**

PALACE DANCERS

507 DESIGN some **BALLET** SHOES.

508 COLOR the **TROPHY**.

509 **TRACE** the LINES to finish the DANCERS.

510 Now **COLOR** them in.

STYLE TRIAL

Use **COLOR** to complete the PATTERNS.

OWL PARTY

516 **DOODLE** details on the **BUNTING**.

517 **COLOR** the **BALLOONS**, using the **COLORED DOTS** as a **GUIDE**.

518 HOW MANY CANDLES are on the cake? WRITE the **ANSWER:** ....

519 JOIN the DOTS to finish the **CAKE**.

520 HOW MANY MICE can you count? WRITE the **ANSWER:** ....

MY EMOTI DESIGNS

DESIGN new EMOTIS for these different THINGS:

521 **CAMPING**

522 **DINOSAUR**

523 **HOMEWORK**

524 **COOKING**

525 CASTLE

526 SCHOOL

527 SURFING

528 SELFIE

WINTER WOOLLIES

FIND the **WORDS** in the **WORD SEARCH.**
WORDS can go DOWN or **ACROSS.**

529 boots

530 coat

531 earmuffs

532 gloves

r	y	h	a	t	z	s	q	r	u
f	g	z	c	r	t	a	b	p	o
e	l	p	s	b	y	t	o	c	r
g	o	n	c	i	a	c	o	a	t
q	v	m	a	m	p	h	t	b	w
z	e	o	r	p	v	e	s	j	o
o	s	f	f	w	d	l	t	z	m
p	r	a	c	r	o	x	p	r	v
i	e	a	r	m	u	f	f	s	u
x	c	m	i	t	t	e	n	s	i

533 hat

534 mittens

535 satchel

536 scarf

537 REARRANGE
the winter **ANAGRAM.**

SWON

SNOW

538 FINISH the
SCARF and **HAT.**

108

IN THE GREENHOUSE

539 **COLOR** the PLANTS.

540 **HOW MANY** SNAILS can you see? WRITE the **ANSWER:** 5

541
DRAW a beautiful FLOWER.

542
COLOR the FLOWER.

543
TRACE the lines to **FINISH** the PEARS.

EMOTI-MAGINATION

SEARCH the PHONE SCREEN for the EMOTIS that look like **THESE:**

the **BOXES** when you **FIND** them.

110

549 mermaid

550 panda

551 unicorn

552 lion

553 Now **COLOR** the **EMOTIS.**

WHOSE EGG?

FOLLOW the **TRAILS** to find out which OWL laid each EGG.

554 555 556

557 **COLOR** the OWLS to match their **EGGS**.

BEAUTIFUL BALLET

Can you find **FIVE DIFFERENCES** between the **SCENES**?

✓ the **BOXES** when you **FIND** them.

 558 [1] 559 [2] 560 [3] 561 [4] 562 [5]

DREAMY JEWELRY

Doodle BEADS, CHARMS, **PENDANTS**, and GEMS to create unique JEWELRY!

563

564

565

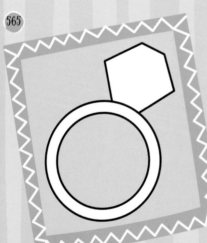

566

567

568

569

570

571

UNICORN MAZE

572 **GUIDE** the **PRINCESS** through the MAZE to reach the **UNICORN**.

573 **COLLECT** all the **FLOWERS** along the way.

Start

Finish

574 **HOW MANY** FLOWERS did you collect?

WRITE the **ANSWER:** ....

TREASURE HUNT

COUNT the **JEWELS** to see who found the MOST treasure.

575 **HOW MANY** JEWELS has HOLLY found? WRITE the ANSWER:

....

576 **HOW MANY** JEWELS has IVY found? WRITE the ANSWER:

....

577 **HOW MANY** JEWELS has DAISY found? WRITE the ANSWER:

....

578 **COLOR** the OWL friends.

PRETTY IN PRINTS

FIND and **CIRCLE** the four **THINGS** that look like **THESE:**

579

580

581

582

SPLISH SPLASH

The **OWLS** are playing in the **RAIN**.
COLOR the UMBRELLAS to keep them DRY.

583

584

585

586 COLOR the falling **RAINDROPS**.

EMOTI-SHIRT

DRAW and **DOODLE** cool **EMOTI** designs on the **T-SHIRTS**.

587

588

589

590

591

592

SUPER MASKS

DESIGN some AWESOME SUPERHERO MASKS!

593

594

595

TIARA TANGLE

DRAW lines to MATCH each PRINCESS to the CORRECT colored **TIARA.**

596

597

598

599

600 **COLOR** the TIARA.

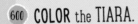

CONNECT THE DOTS

601 **CONNECT** the DOTS to **FINISH** the PICTURE.

602 **DOODLE** details on the **WINGS**.

23 · 24 ·
25 ·
26 · 27 · 28 ·
30 —— 1
29 ·
2 ·
22 ·
21 ·
3 ·
19 ·
5 ·
20 ·
4 ·
18 ·
6 ·
17 ·
7 ·
16 ·
8 ·
15 ·
9 ·
14 ·
10 ·
13 · 12 · 11 ·

603 Now **COLOR** it in.

604 **HOW MANY** FEATHERS can you count? WRITE the **ANSWER:** ....

124

BEAUTIFUL BIRDS

605 DRAW lines to MATCH the **BIRDS** to the correct COLORED **BIRDHOUSES**.

606 COLOR the BIRDS.

607 DECORATE the BIRDHOUSES.

RUNWAY MASTERS

Can you find **TEN** DIFFERENCES between the **SCENES**?
✔ the BOXES when you **FIND** THEM.

608 1   609 2   610 3   611 4   612 5

613 6   614 7   615 8   616 9   617 10

BIRDY BAKERY

618

619

620

DECORATE the owl COOKIES with COLOR and **DOODLES**.

621

EMOTI FUN

DESIGN your own **EMOTIS** for the things you think are really FUN!
Then WRITE the thing in the space BENEATH.

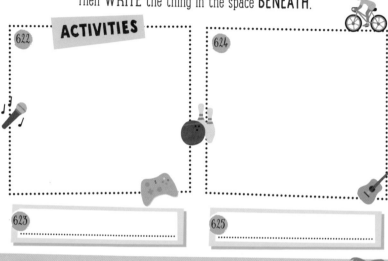

ACTIVITIES

622

624

623

625

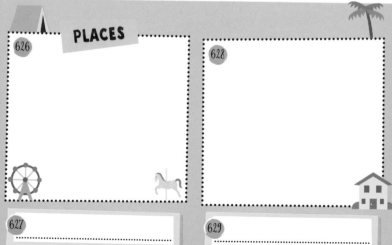

PLACES

626

628

627

629

COOL CAMPING

630 **USE** the **NUMBERS** in the key as a guide to **COLOR** the SCENE.

1 2 3 4

USE COLORS to **FINISH** the camping **ROWS** below.

631

632

633

130

JEWEL MAZE

634 GUIDE the **PRINCE** through the maze to **REACH** the **PRINCESS**.

Start

635 **HOW MANY** GEMS can you count? WRITE the **ANSWER:**

....

Finish

636 **COLOR** the princess's DRESS.

GLITZ BLITZ

ADD COLOR and
DETAILS to the **TIARAS**.

637

638

639

640

641 Can you **FIND** the diamond **RING**?

642 FINISH the SHOES.

643 DESIGN a pretty DRESS.

133

DINER DASH

644 CIRCLE the one that DOESN'T BELONG in a **BURGER**:

Use the **GRID** to FINISH the ITEMS **BELOW**.

DONUT

CUPCAKE

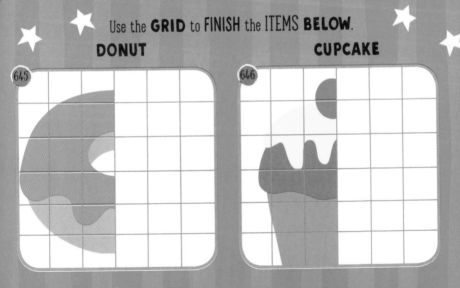

645

646

647 Now **COLOR** the other halves to **MATCH**.

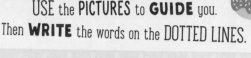

UNSCRAMBLE the WORDS below.
USE the PICTURES to **GUIDE** you.
Then **WRITE** the words on the DOTTED LINES.

OHT GDO

648 ....

KSHIMLEAK

649 ....

650 **JOIN** the **DOTS** to reveal the **PICTURE**.

651 Then **COLOR** it in.

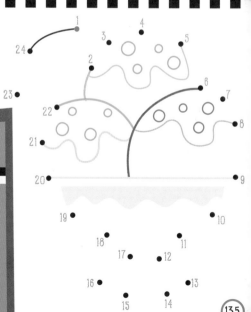

TODAY'S SPECIAL:

i _ e
_ r _ _ m

652 **WRITE** the **MISSING** LETTERS to reveal **TODAY'S SPECIAL**.

(135)

EMOTI NAILS

DESIGN amazing **EMOTI** NAIL ART on each **HAND**.

653

DOODLE some more emoti **BRACELETS** and RINGS.

654

VEGETABLE PATCH

659 **COLOR** the **VEGETABLES**.

CIRCLE the one that **DOESN'T BELONG**:

660

661

662

663

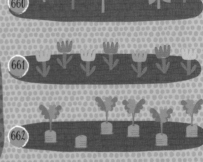

664 **DRAW** your own **VEGETABLE PATCH**.

138

HELP the owl **COUNT** the EGGS.

665

🥚🥚 + 🥚 = ...

666

🥚🥚🥚🥚 + 🥚🥚🥚🥚 = ...

667

🥚🥚🥚🥚 + 🥚🥚 = ...

668

🥚🥚🥚 + 🥚 = ...

669

🥚 + 🥚🥚🥚 = ...

670

🥚🥚🥚🥚 + 🥚🥚🥚 = ...

671

🥚 + 🥚 = ...

672

🥚 + 🥚🥚🥚 = ...

DEER TROUBLE

LOOK at the PICTURES below to **ANSWER QUESTIONS** about the DEER.

673 Who has **GREEN ANTLERS?**

674 Who has **YELLOW HOOVES?**

675 Who has a **PINK NOSE?**

CLARA'S COLLECTIONS

CIRCLE the **ONE** that DOESN'T MATCH in each collection.

676

677

678

679

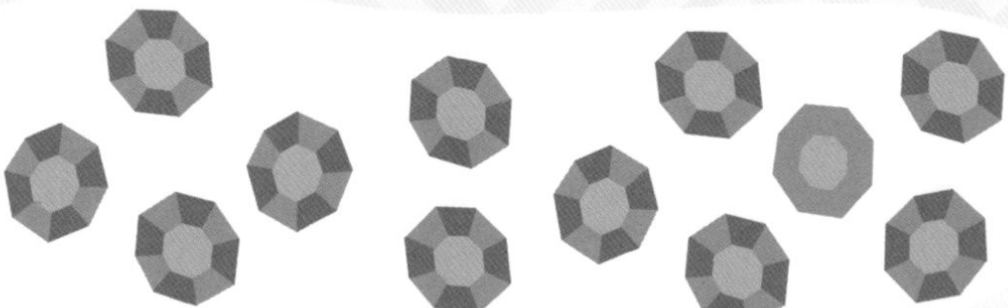

DREAM PETS

In the FRAMES, **DRAW** EMOTIS of your dream PETS.
Then **GIVE** your pets NAMES in the spaces below!

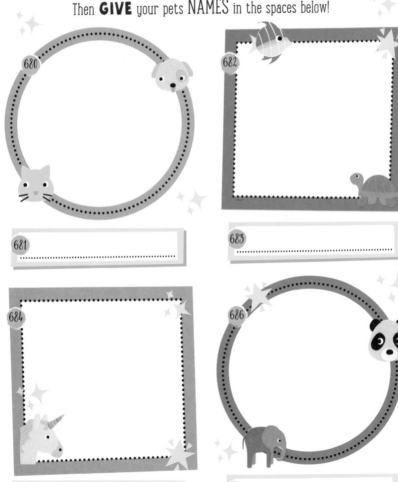

680

681

682

683

684

685

686

687

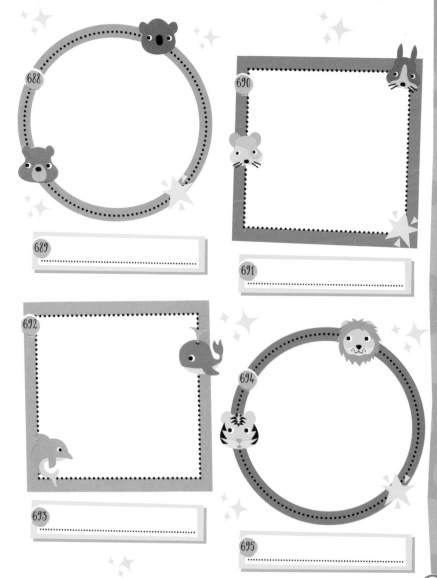

688

689

690

691

692

693

694

695

143

COPY AND COLOR

696 **COLOR** the PICTURE to make it **MATCH** the one OPPOSITE.

144

COUNT the THINGS listed, and then
WRITE the **TOTALS** in the space **BELOW.**

697 **STARS:**

698 **PLANETS:**

699 **OWLS:**

TERRIFIC SNEAKERS

700 **DOODLE** PATTERNS on the sneakers.

701 **CREATE** a MATCHING pair – or dare to be DIFFERENT!

702 **DESIGN** your **PERFECT** shoe.

703 Now **COLOR** it in.

WHO LIVES HERE?

TRACE the TRAILS to find out WHICH owl lives in the **BARN**.

704

705

706

707 **COLOR** the owl FRIENDS.

708 **HOW MANY** FLOWERS can you COUNT? WRITE the ANSWER: ....

BRILLIANT BAKES

DECORATE the COOKIES.

709

710

711

712

713 ✔ the boxes to DESIGN your perfect CAKE.

714 **DRAW** a YUMMY CAKE here.

☐ candles

☐ cherries

☐ chocolate sprinkles

☐ pink frosting

☐ strawberries

☐ white frosting

148

SUPER SNACKS

Search the **GRID** for the **FOOD** words below.
WORDS can go **DOWN** or **ACROSS**.

✓ each WORD when you've **FOUND** IT.

y	i	p	s	b	a	n	a	n	a
a	c	x	t	n	c	m	e	i	l
p	e	p	r	o	h	t	n	w	o
p	c	r	a	y	o	g	u	r	t
l	r	e	w	y	c	d	b	u	z
e	e	t	b	q	o	t	i	b	l
y	a	z	e	u	l	f	c	o	l
e	m	e	r	c	a	k	e	i	r
i	b	l	r	l	t	y	b	r	v
o	c	l	y	o	e	a	z	i	c

715
apple

716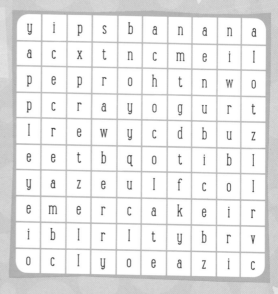
banana

717
cake

718
chocolate

719
ice-cream

720
pretzel

721
strawberry

722
yogurt

149

DRESS TO IMPRESS

723 FINISH the CORSAGE.

724 DECORATE the FAN.

725 **HOW MANY** gold HEARTS can you count? WRITE the ANSWER: ....

726 GIVE this dress **LOTS** of BLING.

EMOTI FAVES

DESIGN EMOTIS for your **FAVORITE** things.
Then **WRITE** what they are in the spaces BELOW.

TREASURES

727

729

728

730

CLOTHES

731

733

732

734

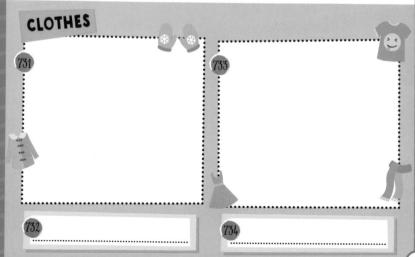

SEE THE SIGHTS

HOW will the girls **TRAVEL** the world? **FOLLOW** the lines to find out.

735

736

737

738 **COLOR** the
HOT-AIR BALLOON.

739 **NAME** your TOP vacation **DESTINATIONS**.

1 ....

2 ....

3 ....

4 ....

5 ....

740 **GIVE** the girl a **COOL** ROAD-TRIP outfit.

741 **DESIGN** a cute **BAG**.

UNDER THE SEA

742 **COLOR** the underwater **PALACE**.

LOOK at the **SCENE**.
✔ the **BOXES**
when you **FIND** the
THINGS listed **BELOW**.

744   2 pink fish ☐

745   3 flags ☐

746   1 whale ☐

747   1 sea horse ☐

743 **HOW MANY**
CROWNS can you count?
WRITE the **ANSWER:** ....

748

749

750

751

5 shells ☐

1 treasure chest ☐

1 dolphin ☐

3 sea stars ☐

ROYAL RAIN

The PRINCESSES are PLAYING in the RAIN.

DRAW FACES on the RAINCLOUDS.

752

753

COLOR the JEWELS on the UMBRELLAS.

754

755

DECORATE the RAINCOATS.

756

757

PRETTY PERCHES

COLOR the BIRDS to match their **PERCHES**.

758

759

760

761

762

763

DOODLE TIME

DOODLE emoti faces in the yellow circles.

764

765

766

767

768

769

770

771

772

158

OWL OPPOSITES

DRAW lines to **MATCH** the OPPOSITES.

773
wet

774
asleep

775
big

776
hot

cold

awake

dry

small

DRESS TO IMPRESS

777 **COLOR** the BAG.

778 **COLOR** the BOW.

779 **DESIGN** a PRETTY party DRESS.

780 **COLOR** the SUNGLASSES to match.

FIND the THREE items that look like THIS:

781

782

783

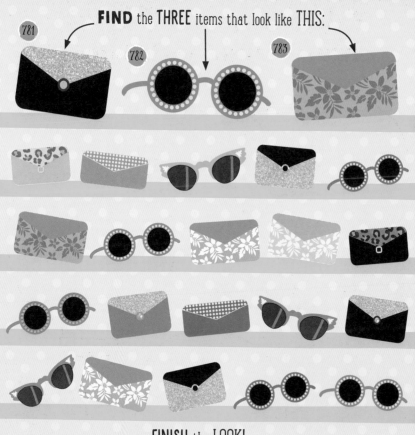

FINISH the LOOK!

784 USE colors to FINISH the SHOES and clutch BAGS.

HIGH IN THE SKY

DOODLE colorful **PATTERNS** on the HOT-AIR BALLOONS.

785

786

787

788 **CIRCLE** the one that DOESN'T BELONG in the **SKY**.

789 **COPY** the **ROCKET.** Use the GRID to help you.

790 Now **COLOR** it in.

GARAGE SALE

SEARCH the **GARAGE SALE** for the ITEMS BELOW. ✓ the **BOXES** when you FIND them.

791 ☐ blue bow   792 ☐ knapsack   793 ☐ pink sunglasses

794 ☐ roller skates   795 ☐ orange mittens   796 ☐ red dress

164

CROWN JEWELS

HELP the princess COUNT the CROWN JEWELS.

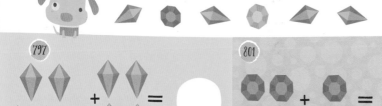

797

 + = ...

801

+ = ...

798

+ = ...

802

+ = ...

799

+ = ...

803

+ = ...

800

 + = ...

804

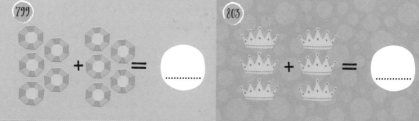 + = ...

EMOTI QUIZ

CIRCLE the **ANSWERS** to the **QUESTIONS** below.

805 **WHICH** EMOTIS are **PETS?**

806 **WHICH** ONE of these **EMOTIS** DOESN'T BELONG?

807 **WHICH** ONE of these emotis is **SLEEPING?**

HEDGE MAZE

FOLLOW the trails to see who **REACHES** the **MIDDLE** of the hedge **MAZE**.

808

809

Finish

810

811

COOL KITES

FOLLOW the lines to see which **KITE** belongs to each **PRINCESS**.

815

814

816 **HOW MANY** STARS can you count? WRITE the **ANSWER:**

....

817 Now **COLOR** the KITES.

SWEET SCENE

LOOK at the SCENE.
✓ the BOXES
when you **FIND** the
THINGS on the list.

818 1 cute deer ☐

819 2 swirly snails ☐

820 2 hiding rabbits ☐

821 3 blue butterflies ☐

822 3 flying owls

823 4 busy bees

824 4 purple flowers

825 6 red apples

UNIQUE UNICORN

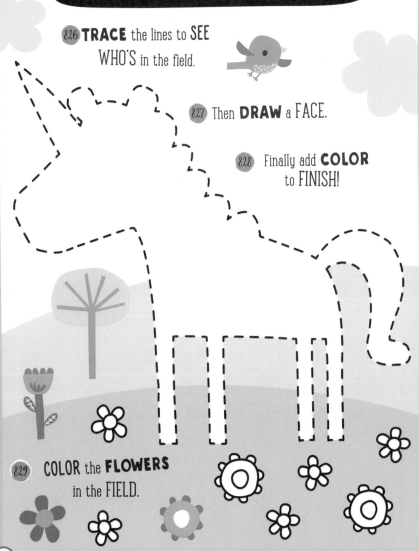

826 **TRACE** the lines to SEE WHO'S in the field.

827 Then **DRAW** a FACE.

828 Finally add **COLOR** to FINISH!

829 COLOR the **FLOWERS** in the FIELD.

EMOTI MADNESS

Use **COLOR** to FINISH the rows, and then
CIRCLE the one that **DOESN'T BELONG** in each ROW.

830

831

832

833

WEDDING STYLE

COLOR and **DOODLE** to design a dream WEDDING.

834 **DESIGN** the ultimate WEDDING SHOES.

835 **FINISH** the BOUQUET.

836 **STYLE** the HAIR.

837 Now **DESIGN** the **DRESS!**

838 **DRAW** your dream **RING**.

839 **DRAW** or **PASTE** a picture of your **BEST FRIEND** as a **BRIDESMAID**.

NIGHT OWLS

FIND SIX OWLS hiding in the scene.

☑ the **BOXES** when you **FIND** them.

- (840) ☐ 1
- (841) ☐ 2
- (842) ☐ 3
- (843) ☐ 4
- (844) ☐ 5
- (845) ☐ 6

(846) **COLOR** the TREES and FLOWERS.

COLOR CLUES

Search the **GRID** for the **COLORS** below.
WORDS can go DOWN or **ACROSS**.

✔ each WORD when you've **FOUND** IT.

w	l	l	o	p	b	q	w	r	e
a	e	o	b	s	l	z	i	k	d
r	a	r	v	p	u	r	p	l	e
e	f	a	n	x	e	a	l	j	y
d	y	n	u	i	l	i	p	l	l
f	u	g	r	e	e	n	n	i	k
g	i	e	x	s	q	b	u	n	f
r	w	q	r	x	a	o	j	k	d
e	y	e	l	l	o	w	r	t	z
m	a	s	r	q	n	m	k	p	o

847

blue

848

green

849
orange

850

pink

851

purple

852
rainbow

853

red

854

yellow

STEP BY STEP

DRAW lines to MATCH each **DANCER** to their **PARTNER**.

855 856 857 858

OODLES OF OWLETS

Use **COLOR** to FINISH the owlet **PATTERNS**.

859

860

861

862

DREAM PHONE

DECORATE your own EMOTI PHONE COVERS.

WRITE **MESSAGES** to your friends on the PHONE SCREENS.
You can **ADD** your fave **EMOTIS,** too.

866

867

868

869

FABULOUS FLOWERS

870 **USE** COLOR to **COMPLETE** the scene.

871
DRAW funny FACES
on the FLOWERS.

872 **HOW MANY**
BEES can you count?
WRITE the **ANSWER**: ....

FANTASTIC FLAGS

USE COLORS to **DECORATE** the FLAGS.

873

874

875

876

877 CIRCLE the **PALACE** that is DIFFERENT.

FAVORITE FEAST

FOLLOW each line to **MATCH** the owls
to their **FAVORITE FOOD.**

878

879

880

881 **COLOR** the yummy **CUPCAKE.**

EMOTI ME

882 **DRAW** YOURSELF as your very own. **UNIQUE EMOTI.**

883 Now **COLOR** it in!

884 **DOODLE** PATTERNS on the picture **FRAME.**

885 **HOW MANY** RED HEARTS can you count? WRITE the **ANSWER:** ....

DAYTIME DESIGNS

FINISH the cool STREET LOOKS.

886

887

888 **DESIGN** a street-style SHIRT.

889 **CREATE** some street ART.

890 **FINISH** the BAG.

891 **ADD** color to this COOL OUTFIT.

ROYAL WORD SEARCH

FIND the **WORDS** in the WORD SEARCH. WORDS can go DOWN or **ACROSS**.

q	a	u	b	p	r	p	h	j	k
s	q	i	r	o	y	a	l	z	o
a	s	e	b	a	l	l	t	r	l
r	t	u	e	q	r	a	j	c	r
t	x	f	m	u	n	c	n	r	e
i	j	w	j	e	w	e	l	o	w
a	u	e	x	e	k	e	b	w	q
r	y	l	b	n	l	p	o	n	y
a	l	a	p	d	j	f	c	o	i
s	o	z	q	f	h	d	v	p	o

 892 ball ✓

 893 crown

 894 jewel ✓

895 palace

 896 pony

 897 queen ✓

 898 royal ✓

 899 tiara

900 HOW MANY JEWELS can you count? WRITE the **ANSWER:** ....

WHAT WAS THAT?

DRAW lines to connect each **CREATURE** to the NOISE it makes.

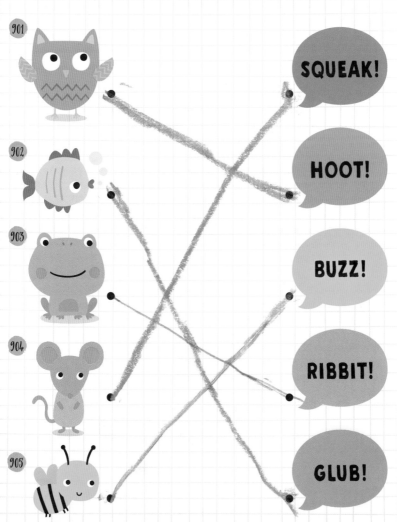

GLORIOUS GOWNS

COLOR and **DECORATE** the **GOWNS** for the princesses.

906

907

908

SNACK TIME

FINISH COLORING the yummy TREATS.

915 **DRAW** your own EMOTI SNACKS here.

PROM PLANNER

916 **WHAT** would the PROM THEME be?

....

....

COLOR the GUESTS
to design a perfect **PROM!**

917

918

919

920 **WHO** would you INVITE?

....

921 WHAT SONG would **PLAY** at the end of the night?

....

922 **DESIGN** your perfect OUTFIT!

WINTER WISHES

Search the **GRID** for the WORDS below.
WORDS can go DOWN or **ACROSS**.

923 **COLOR** the OWL.

d	r	a	g	o	n	f	l	y	c
x	e	u	b	e	e	m	o	i	w
z	g	y	u	x	z	s	w	s	z
l	x	b	t	f	d	n	x	p	i
e	y	i	t	y	c	a	k	i	p
a	q	t	e	q	x	i	c	d	l
f	l	s	r	c	n	l	t	e	b
c	e	m	f	l	o	w	e	r	m
o	s	z	l	q	u	i	k	o	s
u	w	i	y	e	z	t	r	e	e

✔ each WORD when you've **FOUND** IT.

924 ✔
bee

925 ✔
butterfly

926  ✔
dragonfly

927 ✔
flower

928 ✔
leaf

929 ✔
snail

930 ✔
spider

931 ✔
tree

STYLE THE SHOES

DESIGN the emoti **SHOES**. They can both **MATCH** or be completely **DIFFERENT!**

932

933

934 Then **COLOR** them in.

MUDDLED MOMMIES

The **OWLETS** are confused! **DRAW** a LINE
from each OWLET to its **MOMMY**.

935

936

937

938

FILL-IN FACES

DOODLE EMOTI FACES in the yellow **CIRCLES**.

939

940

941

942

943

944

945

946

947

BY THE RIVER

LOOK at the SCENE. ☑ the BOXES when you **FIND** the ANIMALS on the list.

948 2 frogs ☐

949 2 owls ☐

950 3 ducks ☐

951 2 deer ☐

2 ladybugs

5 dragonflies

2 sleeping fish

6 little fish

PONY MAZE

956 **GUIDE** PIA the **PONY** through the maze to reach the **STABLE**.

Start

957 COLOR PIPER the **PONY**.

Finish

958 HOW MANY APPLES can you COUNT? WRITE the **ANSWER:** ....

NAIL SALON

959 PAINT the NAILS a pretty **COLOR.**

960 DOODLE cool DESIGNS on the **NAILS.**

961 FINISH the **RING.**

FAVE CELEBS

In the FRAMES, **DRAW** EMOTIS of your favorite CELEBRITIES.
Then **WRITE** their **NAME** in the spaces beneath.

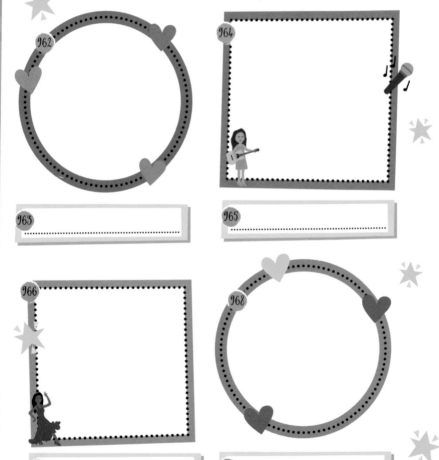

962

963 ....

964

965 ....

966

967 ....

968

969 ....

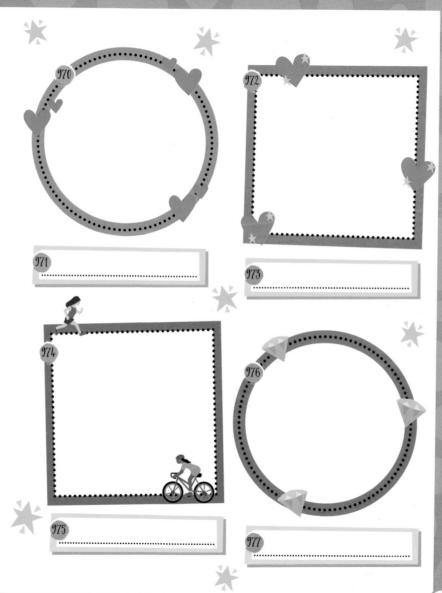

970

971

972

973

974

975

976

977

TOP TOYS

Can you find **FIVE DIFFERENCES** between the **SCENES?**

✓ the boxes when you **FIND** them.

978 | 1   979 | 2   980 | 3   981 | 4   982 | 5

PRINCESS PARTY

983 **COLOR** the **BUNTING**.

984 **HOW MANY** CUPCAKES can you see? WRITE the **ANSWER:** ....

985 **COLOR** the **PRESENT** to make it **MATCH**.

SUMMER FUN

FIND all **EIGHT EMOTIS** in the grid.
WORDS can go **DOWN** or **ACROSS**.

986 cycling

987 dress

988 flowers

989 pineapple

s	x	t	c	y	c	l	i	n	g
u	t	e	j	u	d	r	e	s	s
n	v	n	x	n	k	z	c	y	a
g	y	n	l	o	e	k	e	c	n
l	o	i	t	s	h	e	l	l	d
a	p	s	w	q	c	s	x	f	a
s	k	o	t	x	j	l	y	n	l
s	f	l	o	w	e	r	s	g	s
e	i	y	h	m	k	q	r	c	y
s	p	i	n	e	a	p	p	l	e

990 sandals

991 shell

992 sunglasses

993 tennis

994 Use **COLOR** to **DECORATE** the BUTTERFLY SCENE.

ROYAL ROWS

CIRCLE the **THING** that **DOESN'T BELONG** in each row.

995

996

997

998

999 **FINISH** the rows with **COLOR.**

TIME FOR BED

1,000

COLOR the SCENE.